Meet...

the Flying Doctors

WRITTEN BY GEORGE IVANOFF

ILLUSTRATED BY BEN WOOD

RANDOM HOUSE AUSTRALIA

For my daughter Lexi, with whom sharing picture books is one of my greatest delights. GI

For the Blanch family — there are three of us in this book! BW

A Random House book
Published by Penguin Random House Australia Pty Ltd
Level 3, 100 Pacific Highway, North Sydney NSW 2060
penguin.com.au

Penguin
Random House
Australia

First published by Random House Australia in 2016
This edition published by Random House Australia in 2017

National Library of Australia
Cataloguing-in-Publication entry

Author: Ivanoff, George, author
Title: Meet . . . the Flying Doctors / George Ivanoff; illustrated by Ben Wood
ISBN: 978 0 14378 067 0 (paperback)
Series: Meet; 12
Target Audience: For primary school age
Subjects: Flynn, John, 1880–1951
Royal Flying Doctor Service of Australia
Medical emergencies – Juvenile literature
Airplane ambulances – Australia – Juvenile literature
Other Creators/Contributors: Wood, Ben, 1983– illustrator
Dewey Number: 362.180994

Cover and internal illustrations by Ben Wood
Cover and internal design by Christabella Designs
Printed in China

For education materials and fun ideas visit: flyingdoctor4education.org.au/

RFDS stands for Royal Flying Doctor Service.
It is a not-for-profit organisation that provides
emergency and primary health care across Australia.
This is the story of how the life-saving service was
created and grew to become an Australian icon.

There's this man on the $20 note.
His name is Reverend John Flynn,
and he saved my life.

He died in 1951, long before
I was born.

So how could he save my life?
That's a long story. A story
that begins in 1911.

In 1911 John Flynn came to work at a mission in Beltana, a small settlement more than 500 kilometres north of Adelaide.

John saw that the people of this remote area had no proper medical care. The nearest doctor was days away. It was even further to the nearest hospital.

John started to think about what could be done. A few years later he was inspired by a very sad story.

In 1917 a stockman named James Darcy was mustering cattle at Ruby Plains, in the Kimberley region of Western Australia. He fell from his horse and was badly hurt.

He was taken to the closest town, Halls Creek, by horse and buggy. The journey took 12 hours. There was no hospital or doctor, so James was brought to the postmaster, who knew some first aid.

The postmaster telegraphed Perth for medical advice.

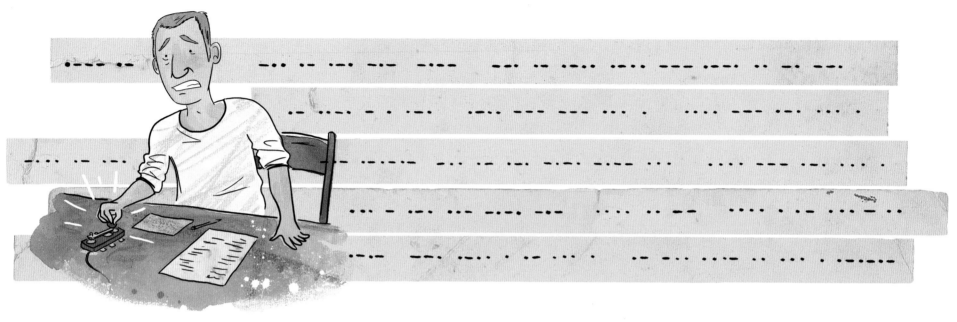

A doctor responded and made his diagnosis through telegraph messages – a series of morse code dots and dashes zipping back and forth along the wires. James had internal injuries and would need an operation straight away.

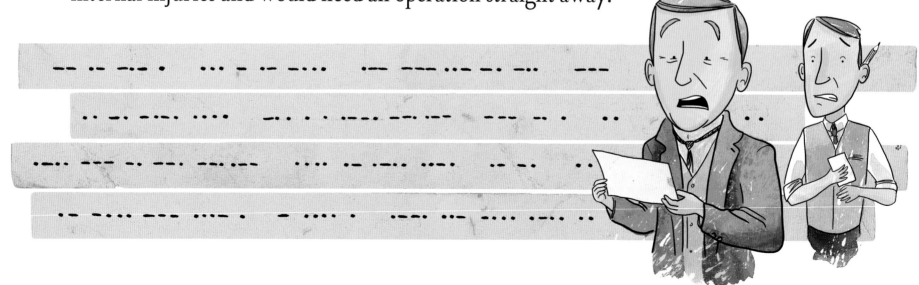

The doctor sent instructions so the postmaster could do the operation.

The postmaster had only a razor and a penknife to operate with.

The postmaster operated on James for seven hours. But James didn't get better. So the doctor set off for Halls Creek.

His journey took thirteen days, and he travelled by boat,

car and finally a horse and sulky.

He arrived in Halls Creek one day too late to help poor James Darcy.

John Flynn read about James Darcy in a newspaper. The story showed how important it was to get medical care to outback areas.

That same year, John Flynn received a letter from a young Victorian pilot who was serving in the First World War. The pilot suggested that aeroplanes could be used to fly doctors around the outback.

John Flynn had already been thinking of using planes. The pilot helped
Flynn work out the details.

Flynn began a campaign to form a medical organisation that would use planes.
It took ten years to get enough support, but finally he put his plans into motion.

In 1928 John formed the Australian Inland Mission Aerial Medical Service, or AMS. The AMS used a single engine de Havilland biplane, named *Victory*, which was leased from QANTAS.

The first flight was on 17 May. *Victory* flew 137 kilometres from the AMS base in Cloncurry, Queensland, to Julia Creek. More than 100 people were there to meet the plane.

By the end of its first year, the AMS had made 50 flights and treated 255 patients.

There was no radio in the *Victory*. All the pilot had to help with navigation was a compass. He had to find his way by looking for landmarks such as fences, rivers, roads and telegraph lines.

Navigating in this way was difficult work and meant that flights were mostly made during daylight hours. Night flights were only made in cases of extreme urgency.

Nowadays RFDS planes use satellite navigation systems. The planes usually land on airstrips or roads. Most large cattle stations have an airstrip.

R.F.D.S. EMERGENCY
AIRSTRIP

But the *Victory* and the other early planes landed in all sorts of places, from claypans to hastily cleared paddocks.

When the *Victory* first started flying its missions, calls for help were sent by telegraph. Many remote areas did not have access to telegraph services.

Over the years, new technology helped people contact the service. Pedal-powered radios were developed and placed in remote communities from 1929. These radios allowed people in areas with no electricity or telegraph wires to call the RFDS for help.

Voice radios and batteries made it even easier to communicate from the mid-1930s.

Now, we have satellite phones.

John Flynn's Aerial Medical Service was so successful that it expanded to the other states from 1934.

Its name has changed over the years too. In 1955 Queen Elizabeth II granted the service a royal charter. It became the Royal Flying Doctor Service (RFDS).

Of course, the Flying Doctors weren't all doctors and pilots. Sister Myra Blanch became the first nurse to work with the RFDS in 1945. Although she sometimes flew in place of a doctor, she mostly gave health talks over the radio and made visits by road to the Tibooburra area in New South Wales.

The nurses took to the air full-time in the 1960s and were given
the official title of 'Flight Sisters'.

The first Flight Sister was Marie Osborn,
who went on missions from Derby.

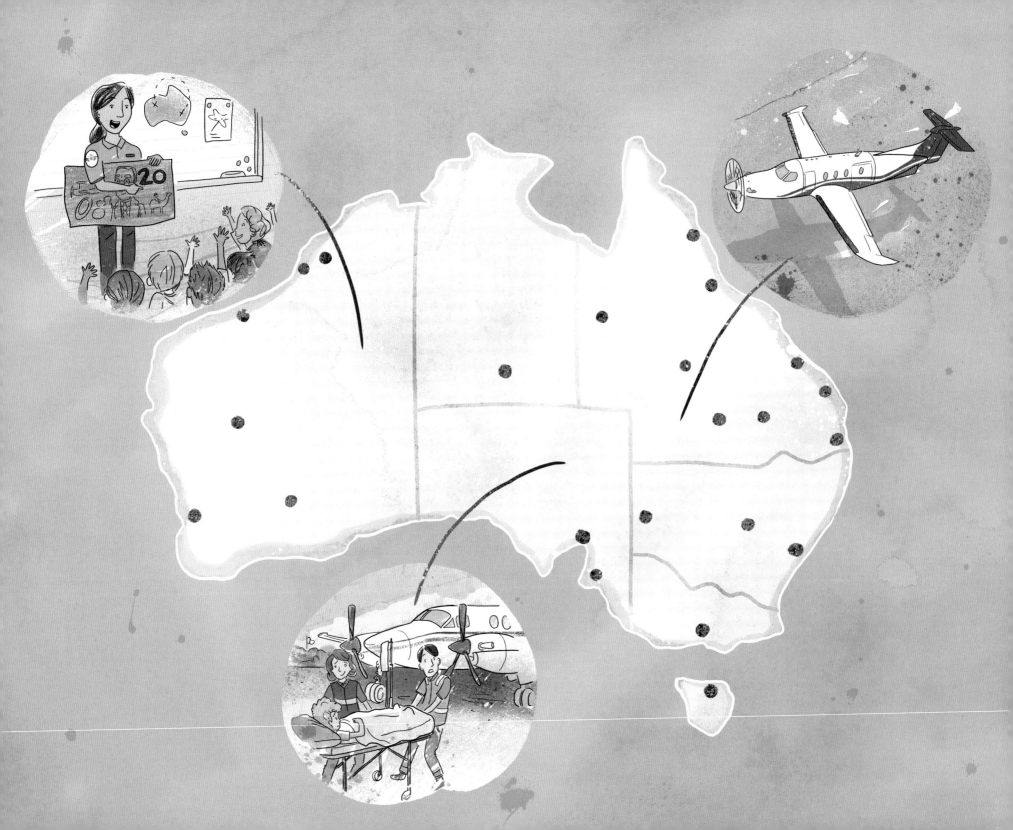

Reverend John Flynn died in 1951, but the RFDS is still going strong. It now has a fleet of 66 planes, operating from 23 bases across the country. The service runs clinics in towns with no doctor, provides dental care where there are no dentists, and teaches people about health and nutrition.

I suppose you're wondering what all of that has got to do with me.

My family lives on a sheep farm in the middle of South Australia. When I got really sick, an RFDS plane brought a doctor to see me at the farm.

And that's how Reverend John Flynn saved my life.

Timeline

1880 (25 November): John Flynn is born at Moliagul in central Victoria. His parents are school teacher Thomas Eugene and Rosetta Flynn.

1898–1903: John Flynn is a school teacher with the Victorian Education Department.

1903–1907: Flynn begins training for the ministry, serving as a 'Home Missionary' to remote communities in rural Victoria. He witnesses the harshness of bush life and is moved by the struggles of the people.

1907: John Flynn begins formal divinity studies at Ormond College at the University of Melbourne.

1911 (24 January): John Flynn is ordained as a Minister of the Presbyterian Church.

1911 (February): John Flynn comes to work at the Smith of Dunesk Mission in Beltana, north of Adelaide in South Australia. He starts laying the foundations of a medical service, setting up bush hospitals staffed by nurses in remote areas of Australia where there is no medical care.

1912: John Flynn presents a report to the Presbyterian Church, which results in the creation of the Australian Inland Mission. Flynn is appointed head of this organisation. He recruits the first of his team of 'roving padres', who travel on camel to visit isolated homesteads.

1917 (August): Stockman James Darcy falls from his horse in the Western Australian outback. He is transported to the nearest town and operated on by the postmaster, WJ Tuckett, but dies before the doctor assisting via telegraph, Dr John Holland, can get to him. This story inspires John Flynn.

1917 (20 November): Lieutenant Clifford Peel, a Victorian pilot, writes a letter to John Flynn. Peel outlines how aircraft could be used to fly doctors around the outback.

1926: Hugh Victor McKay – industrialist, childhood friend, strong supporter of Flynn's scheme – dies. He leaves a bequest that will enable an aerial medical service to be set up in Cloncurry. The service is set up as a one-year trial.

1928: The Australian Inland Mission Aerial Medical Service (AMS) is established in Cloncurry, Queensland.

1928 (27 March): The AMS signs a contract with QANTAS for the lease of a single engine de Havilland biplane.

1928 (15 May): The AMS's first doctor, Dr Kenyon St Vincent Welch, arrives at the Cloncurry base.

1928 (17 May): First AMS flight. Pilot Arthur Affleck flies Dr Kenyon St Vincent Welch 137 km from the AMS base in Cloncurry to Julia Creek.

1929: Radio equipment and operator are installed at Cloncurry base. Engineer Alfred Traeger starts producing pedal-operated sets, which are distributed to surrounding communities so they can call for the doctor.

1930s: During the Great Depression, government funding for the AMS is cut and donations dwindle. The service comes to the brink of closing altogether, but is saved by the skilful efforts of Flynn and his helpers, who manage to expand the service, despite the difficult economic climate.

1933: John Flynn is appointed an officer of the Order of the British Empire.

1934: The Australian Inland Mission hands over the running of the AMS to a newly formed organisation called the Australian Aerial Medical Service (AAMS). A second base is opened in Western Australia. John Flynn's vision of a national service is beginning to be realised.

1936: A film called *The Flying Doctor* is released in Australia. It is a fictional story about a man who becomes a flying doctor in the Australian outback. It leads to an increase in donations to the Australian Aerial Medical Services.

1937: John Flynn marries Jean Baird, the secretary of the Australian Inland Mission.

1940–1945: During World War II, flying doctor planes are requisitioned for the war. There are shortages of doctors, pilots, nurses and equipment. The northern bases are moved due to bombing and the radio network used for defence.

1940: The AAMS buys its first plane, a de Havilland DH.84 Dragon. All previous planes had been leased.

1942: The Australian Aerial Medical Service is renamed the Flying Doctor Service of Australia (FDS).

1945: Sister Myra Blanch becomes the first nurse to be employed by the FDS.

1950: First School of the Air session is broadcast from the FDS Alice Springs base.

1951 (5 May): John Flynn dies of cancer in Sydney.

1955: The Flying Doctor Service receives a royal charter and becomes the Royal Flying Doctor Service of Australia (RFDS).

1960: Nurse Marie Osborne becomes the first Flight Sister employed by the RFDS.

1985 (March): *The Flying Doctors* three-episode mini series, based on the activities of the real RFDS, screens on Australian television. Its popularity leads to the production of a television series that runs for nine seasons until 1992. An additional series called *RFDS* is then made the following year. These television adaptations raise the profile of the RFDS in Australia and overseas, leading to an increase in donations to the RFDS.

2009: The RFDS gets its first jet aircraft, a Hawker 800XP.

2016: In 2016, the RFDS assists more than 290,000 patients through emergency aeromedical visits; nurse, GP and dental clinics; patient road and air transport and the RFDS telehealth services via radio, telephone, email, fax and video.

The *Meet . . .* series

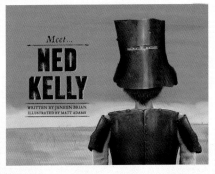

Meet...
NED KELLY
WRITTEN BY JANEEN BRIAN
ILLUSTRATED BY MATT ADAMS

Meet...
Mary MacKillop
WRITTEN BY SALLY MURPHY
ILLUSTRATED BY SONIA MARTINEZ

Meet...
CAPTAIN COOK
WRITTEN BY RAE MURDIE
ILLUSTRATED BY CHRIS NIXON

Meet...
the ANZACS
WRITTEN BY CLAIRE SAXBY
ILLUSTRATED BY MAX BERRY

Meet...
DOUGLAS MAWSON
WRITTEN BY MIKE DUMBLETON
ILLUSTRATED BY SNIP GREEN

Meet...
Nancy Bird Walton
WRITTEN BY GRACE ATWOOD
ILLUSTRATED BY HARRY SLAGHEKKE

Meet...
BANJO PATERSON
WRITTEN BY KRISTIN WEIDENBACH
ILLUSTRATED BY JAMES GULLIVER HANCOCK

Meet...
WEARY DUNLOP
WRITTEN BY CLAIRE SAXBY
ILLUSTRATED BY JEREMY LORD

Meet...
SIDNEY NOLAN
WRITTEN BY YVONNE MES
ILLUSTRATED BY SANDRA ETEROVIC

Meet...
DON BRADMAN
WRITTEN BY CORAL VASS
ILLUSTRATED BY BRAD HOWE

Meet...
Nellie Melba
WRITTEN BY JANEEN BRIAN
ILLUSTRATED BY CLAIRE MURPHY

Meet...
the Flying Doctors
WRITTEN BY GEORGE IVANOFF
ILLUSTRATED BY BEN WOOD